'Walter Not-A-Wizard'
An original concept by Steve Howson
© Steve Howson 2022

Illustrated by Lilia Miceli

Published by MAVERICK ARTS PUBLISHING LTD
Studio 11, City Business Centre, 6 Brighton Road,
Horsham, West Sussex, RH13 5BB
© Maverick Arts Publishing Limited February 2022
+44 (0)1403 256941

A CIP catalogue record for this book is available at the British Library.

ISBN 978-1-84886-858-8

www.maverickbooks.co.uk

This book is rated as: Gold Band (Guided Reading)

Walter
Not-A-Wizard

by Steve Howson

illustrated by
Lilia Miceli

Chapter 1

In the faraway land of Wazzam, everyone was a wizard. Everyone... except Walter.

Walter's potions were positively powerless.

His spelling was always a muddle.

His charms were utterly charmless.

His curses were totally harmless.

In every wizarding test, Walter scored zero.

Magic came naturally to everyone in Wazzam.

Everyone... except Walter.

So while his friends were learning how to use magic to make castles and feasts and dragons, Walter had other ideas...

He read history books about the time before magic. He learned how people had once built their own homes and grown their own food. He made vast buildings out of wooden blocks. He drew plans for incredible machines and made them from bits of metal and wood and junk. He found seeds and planted them at the bottom of the garden to see what would grow.

His mum and dad worried about Walter's strange behaviour. So did his teachers. They worried that he had no magical skills. How would he pass his school magic tests? They wondered what he would do when he grew up.

How could a person without any magic live happily in the land of Wazzam?

"Don't worry about me," said Walter. "People lived without magic before. I can be just like them."

His mum and dad shook their heads sadly.

Chapter 2

Soon, the chief wizards of Wazzam found out about Walter. He was summoned by the mighty wizards: Bibbi and Bobbi and Boo.

"We are worried about you, Walter," said Bibbi.

"You are the first Not-A-Wizard in Wazzam for more than 100 years," said Bobbi.

"We do not know how you can stay in Wazzam without magic," said Boo.

"It's fine," said Walter. "I've read all about it. I don't need any magic, thank you."

"Pah! Nonsense!" huffed Bibbi.

"Where will you live?" said Bobbi.

"I'm going to build my own house," said Walter. "Did you know, there used to be lots of little cottages in Wazzam, before the wizards turned them all into castles? I'm going to make one of those."

"What will you eat?" asked Boo.

"I'm going to grow my own food, just like they did in the olden days," said Walter.

"Without magic?" said Bibbi. "Impossible!"

"We will be watching you very closely indeed, young man," said Bobbi.

Chapter 3

Walter made the tools he needed. He carved rocks into building blocks. He gathered wood and made it into doors and window frames. He designed a machine to lift the heavy stones into place.

"What a waste of time," said Bobbi.

It took Walter many months to finish the job. But when it was done, he had a cosy little cottage to live in.

"Now I'm going to grow my own food," said Walter.

"You can't grow food," said Boo. "You make food with magic."

Walter gathered seeds and plants from the woods. He dug the soil, sowed the seeds, and watered them every day. Eventually, he had a fine garden full of fruit and vegetables.

"Yuck!" said Boo. "Who would eat food made out of soil?"

Walter's mum and dad were very proud of his achievements. They held a little party on the day Walter moved into his new home. Walter made a feast from the food he had grown.

To everyone's surprise, it was delicious!

Chapter 4

Then something odd began to happen in Wazzam. A strange feeling came over all the wizards. They felt dizzy and confused. One by one, they began to lose their magical powers.

The wizards found they could no longer conjure up amazing animals, or fly from place to place, or create potions to make them feel better.

Their magical castles turned back into simple cottages. But there were holes in the roofs and the windows were missing.

In the middle of all the crumbling cottages stood Walter's tidy little house and garden. Walter felt very sorry for all his wizard friends and family. He wanted to help them. But the chief wizards were angry.

"Your 'Not-A-Wizard' disease has spread to all of us," said Bibbi.

"Now none of us has any magic," said Bobbi. "You will have to leave the land of Wazzam immediately. Then perhaps your 'Not-A-Wizard' disease will go away."

"...Could I have an apple, please?" said Boo.

"Yes," said Walter. "You can all have some food if you're hungry. I could show you how to grow it, if you like. And how to repair your houses."

Chapter 5

So Walter taught the wizards how to fix their homes and how to grow real food.

The people of Wazzam had never used their hands to make things before. They made lots of mistakes. And they got cross.

But they learned because they had to. Magic could not help them anymore.

Walter's wisdom spread far and wide.
Ruined cottages were turned into cosy
homes all over the land. Gardens full of
vegetables and fruit grew up everywhere.

The wizards found that they loved to build
with their hands and grow their own food.
It felt good.

Soon the wizards of Wazzam began to feel better. The dizziness went away. They started to feel stronger and healthier.

Then, just as mysteriously as it had vanished, their magic returned.

The wizards found they were fizzing with magical energy once more.

Chapter 6

But the wizards had changed. They knew what it was like to live without magic. So they kept their real houses made from real stones, and their real food grown in the soil.

They decided to use their magical powers for less important things, like entertaining each other, hosting amazing parties or putting on huge firework displays.

The biggest party they organised was for Walter. But instead of conjuring up a magical feast, everyone brought along the food they had grown themselves. They prepared the most incredible banquet to thank Walter for showing them how to live happily without magic.

Bibbi and Bobbi and Boo announced that Walter would join the chief wizards. He would become the first Chief Not-A-Wizard of Wazzam. His amazing skills would be taught in every school in the land.

And so, in the faraway land of Wazzam, the wisdom of Walter Not-A-Wizard lived on forever.

The End

Book Bands for Guided Reading

The Institute of Education book banding system is a scale of colours that reflects the various levels of reading difficulty. The bands are assigned by taking into account the content, the language style, the layout and phonics. Word, phrase and sentence level work is also taken into consideration.

Maverick Early Readers are a bright, attractive range of books covering the pink to white bands. All of these books have been book banded for guided reading to the industry standard and edited by a leading educational consultant.

Pink
Red
Yellow
Blue
Green
Orange
Turquoise
Purple
Gold
White

To view the whole Maverick Readers scheme, visit our website at
www.maverickearlyreaders.com

Or scan the QR code above to view our scheme instantly!